Love Worth Remembering

Poems of Love and Longing

Ian Lewis

ISBN-13: 9798797726197
ISBN-10: 1477123456

Cover design by: Art Painter
Library of Congress Control Number: 2018675309
Printed in the United States of America

To Thom

Contents

Introduction

This is a collection of poetry written during the beginning of a relationship. Is there a more romantic time in one's life? Is there a more exquisite experience than the first few steps along the journey of love and passion? Once Cupid's arrows have hit, all we want is to escape the ordinary and enjoy the romantic, passionate moments when high desires soar and the visions of love become most vibrant. So gather your lover close and discover yet again how beautiful and sublime new love can be, in these poignant love poems.

I Want To Live With You

I want to live with you completely,
And be with you in every way,
all the time, everywhere.

I'm not talking about just hours with you,
but to be with you all night and all day,
and to breath the same air as you do.

I want to be that close to you forever,
and to share all that lies ahead,
my life, my future, forever!

Take Your Shadow

Take your shadow,
And touch it with light;
Give it a purpose,
And infuse it with flight.

Decorate your days,
With designs that you like;
Say, "I've never been so happy,"
And, "It's never been so right."

Open your windows,
And welcome the light;
Open your heart,
To Love's delight!

We

We get along so very well
and so easily together.

It's just like the two of us
were meant to be together.

I Know I Have Loved You

I know I have loved you many times before;
In many forms, in many ways,
Through many lives,
We've stared into each other's eyes.
--And the memory is there still!

Like soft, sweet words
That are only spoken by true lovers,
Throughout the ages, in all tongues,
Our spirits have reappeared
--We have lived on and on!

We are the love odes of old
And the ballads that chronicle
The joys and the pain of love,
Of separation and union of lovers.
--We are every love that's ever been!

If I stare at you long enough
I know your ancient images will emerge;
I will see you clad in gown and flowers
With the light of time shining from your hair.
--The image of what is remembered forever!

It Was You

It was *you* I have longed for,
While shedding so many tears;
It was *you* I have waited for,
For so many, many years.

It was always *you*,
Even before you came along;
I have heard your tune,
Playing inside every love song.

Yes, *you* are the one,
I have wished for;
And desired, and required;
The one I have always adored.

That Fateful Night

That fateful night I met you,
I saw a shooting star.
It streaked from out of nowhere,
To fall not very far.

It landed in a blaze of fire,
And I ran toward the sound it made:
Like crashing cymbals that gave off light,
It was not shy or staid.

I saw intense white light,
And like neon written was this plea:
"She is the one you've longed for,
She is your wife to be."

I Would Not Resist

I would not resist getting older,
If I could have you always by my side,
Along with all your sweet love until I die.

The years would pass joyful and full,
With your hand always touching mine,
And then, I would thankfully say good-bye.

I cannot ask more of life,
Than what you've brought to me;
And I cannot conceive of a better wife,
With more grace, love, and inner beauty.

So Many

So many *I love you's* were there,
But they were never said.
They were always there,
But they were caught,
Inside my throat.

Yes, so many, many *I love you's*,
Were there inside my mouth,
Until it finally swelled up,
Opened up, poured out,
For the world to see.

My Dear, Behold

My dear, behold,
As Venus in her temple,
You are the object,
Of pure ardent love,
That is all embracing,
That is everlasting,
To this true disciple,
To this passioned worshiper...
Me!

Perfect, Imperfect

You are perfect, my dear.

You are so beautiful
when we meet for our dates and events.
You are so much fun to be with
and so full of life.
You are always happy to see me
and so playfully bright.

You are a perfect lover, my dear.

You are a passionate,
creative lover that is eager and willing.
You have been receptive and responsive,
tireless and accommodating.
You've been forthright
and innocent in equal measures.

You are celebrations, my dear.

You are all good times.
You are weekends and days off.
You are extra special times and events.
You are luxuries and indulgences.
You are tree fruit out of season.
You are a birthday surprise.
You are a summer's day in fall.
You are a twenty dollar bill
found in a pocket of an old coat.

You are all those things and more.
You are special things,
but not everyday reality.

I want everyday reality!

I want the imperfections of life as you.
I don't want to reserve you
as an interruption to my life,
I want you as my life.

You can be imperfect, my dear.

I want to stumble over you
as I get up each morning.
I want to leave my sink messy
and not worry about it.
I want you to do the same.
I want to not treat you as a guest.

You can be for imperfect times, my dear.

I want the luxury of not having to
look forward to seeing you only on special days.
I want to make you my routine.
I want to share regular things and everyday events.
I want to talk about the news
and what the weather will be like tomorrow.

You can be for imperfect reasons, my dear.

I want to share minor crisis and calamities.
I want to tend to your cuts and blisters,
know your children's problems
and know what is going on at your work.
I want you to get upset at me
because I didn't take the trash out
or pick up the bread that I promised I would.

You can be for imperfect relations, my dear.

I want you to focus your love
and attention on me,
but I also want you to make me a habit
that you sometimes forget about.
I want you to occasionally finish my thoughts
or my sentences.
I want you to see me as an extension of you.
And, I want to feel that same way about you.

I don't want a perfect date.

I want a close, loving, real, imperfect wife.

My Love

My love,
You're blessed
With amber eyes,
And you project them
All around, all the time
As you walk and as you talk,
With me my loveliness, with me.

They're still there,
Under your closed lids,
Your fabled amber eyes,
That shine in my memory,
Through every restless breath,
Through each moment of the night:
Your fabled amber eyes are just for me.

Sometimes I Need

Sometimes I need the feel
of your loving hand in mine,
to comfort, to support, to lift me,
and after that --all the world is fine.

I Want So Much

I want so much to reassure you,
That I'm the man you want me to be;
I want to show that I can comfort you,
By doing that which is the way with me.

To the man who hovers over you at night,
(In the dark he can be seen,
leaning in as you dream)
I want to say, "Go now, it's all right,
-- She's happy and will live now
in the way that you deem."

You awoke as he went then,
perhaps for the last time,
And were comforted
by somehow knowing, as was I
Of what had happened
and the sense that all was fine;
-- And the light from the sun
shone extra bright in the sky!

My Prayers

My prayers have been answered
by you.

And with you I will stay
always,
kissing your hair,
caressing your face,
locked in passion,
locked in love's embrace.

You Kissed Someone

You kissed someone coyly in the early spring,
Another kissed you boldly in the early fall;
But the love I bring is not a passing fling,
It will stand and stay for the seasons all!

When The Day

When the day
sheds light
and breaks the night sky
you will be there
close to my heart
and close to my side.

A kiss to start
and "I love you" to say
and that kiss in my mind
will replay through the day.
A passionate tumble
of love displayed,
not quick,
but neither delayed.

Then off we go
to our separate lives
in love's afterglow.

Throughout the long day
you come to mind,
your gentle touch,
your words
so kind,
till the sun goes down,
and we join again
and I place my lips

where my mind has been.

Embraced in love,
our day is done
We lie together,
until the next sun.

The Dew

Have you ever listened to the dew?
It whispers dear,
and delicately of you.

I Want Us To Have

I want us to have a greeting card life;
Me as your loving husband and you as my wife.

Don't you want that too?

Then it's up to us to do it.

Together we can make it all come true!

I See People

I see people on the streets,
and in stores and in cars,
and know they can't possibly be
as happy as you've made me.

I was once like them,
just going through life;
Now I shine, strut and beam:
a man who's finally found his dream.

We Talked

We talked about everything,
As we talked away the day,
We told each other what we had done,
And put our whole lives on display.

We shared moments of our lives,
That were proudest and most profound.
We also shared the saddest days,
That memory still stingingly astound.

After a certain point it became clear,
That we seemed half of a single soul,
That somehow wandered far and near,
Before meeting to finally make it whole.

Though different scars may mark us
And differences may abound,
We each know each other's secrets,
And where we now are bound.

Something

Something went singing,
Like a cannonball through the air,
Toward a far horizon,
To land far away somewhere.

Fireworks went soaring,
Toward their celestial height,
Far beyond the boring,
For I found my love tonight!

The Heartache of Love

The heartache of love:
Does run the heart,
And rule the mind;
I am heavy
With its special kind.

The sense of love:
We never know,
What it has to say;
Though we shouldn't,
Let that drive us away.

The celebration of love:
Loin and tongue,
Do wait for it;
And our bodies
Lust and ache for it.

The communion of love:
Happens only once,
If it occurs at all;
It will be our hearts
Who will hear the call.

We Made Love

We made love on an Autumn eve,
And suddenly darkness disappeared:
Minutes changed to hours,
And love conquered all we feared.

The moon was full and shining,
With the gleam of a special light,
And the earth seemed new, as reborn,
For only us that special night.

Our bed was perched on a hill,
Atop tall timber in the snow;
Below us lay icy meadows,
Buried deep in perfect drifts that glowed.

The cold outside was never felt,
As love kept us warm all night;
We held hands as we talked of plans,
And basked in love's pure and warm delight.

I Have Known

I have known days of every kind,
Some that were mild and friendly,
And some were of that other kind.

Without a singular event to stir me in some way,
All that I remember is
That I've lived through just another numbered day.

But now the numbers one, zero, one, zero,
Are etched in my memory,
When fate brought me to you on that special date.

The Only One

The only one I see is you;
And you rule my world,
With regal majesty.

The only sounds I hear are yours;
Your sweet voice is heard,
As a Mozart melody.

Is there another soul like yours?
So gentle, loving and kind?
Oh no, an impossibility!

We...

came together,
two separate people
with two separate lives,
and two separate everything
and wanted it all to become one.
But was there too much of everything,
with just too many bad memories,
of so many, *many* bad people,
and too many bad lies
for the two of us
for that now?

My Heart

My heart has been seized
by your beauty!
Oh, your power overwhelms
and disarms me.
Will you always please
and make me feel at ease?
I am fragile and faultless.

You, inspiring being,
have won my mind and spirit.
Though my vigilant eye
looks upon you with fright,
each and every night,
I sleep peacefully
knowing you are the one
who is right
to the end of my life
for me.

Freely and willingly
you render your soul to me,
and save your amorous glances
for me.

Oh, you make my limbs weak!
Every whim
that you desire
I will inspire to provide.

Please take me once more
in your embrace
and to your heart.

Spectacular peaks
we will climb.
I only wish to spend
every moment of time with you.
Please don't delay
or betray our happiness.
You are the one
who makes my every day
grow brighter and clearer.

The time spent together is full
of excitement and anticipation
knowing this way
of living will bring
happiness and joy.
You have been sent to me
to be the center
of my universe.

Through you the world is pure
and you open my eyes to new
and adventurous ways.
Provide me with dignity and pride.
Be my only guide for this
and lead me to a new world of
optimism and enthusiasm for life.
Be my wife!

My eyes will see and feel
the sumptuous and wondrous
world of nature.
Birds singing songs of love
will make a dream of

wondrous worlds above
watching and observing life
at its best.

Make my mind feel at rest.
Let me smell the sweet aroma
of blooming flowers
that devour all my tragic hours of misery.
There is beauty all around you.
I breath it in the clean fresh air.

Fully aware am I
of all the pleasures
that you bestow upon me.
Tasting the sweet delectable nature
and feeling of the land as it
touches the soul
I am you.

I know through you I will move
closer to greener
fields of wonderment
where nothing can ever compare
to its brilliant and vibrant
passions of love.

As they embrace each other
their minds and souls face
and feel things no other mortal
could possibly imagine.

Our love will endure forever.
For we are the only two
who know
why we are here.

Describing

Describing the love,
I have for you,
Is deficient,
When I say, "I love you."

It is like a gnat,
Standing in for a tall giraffe:
It is small, so very small,
of all that it really is.

I Know

I know I have loved you many times before;
In many forms, in many ways,
Through many lives;
I've stared into those eyes before,
--And the memory is there still!

Like soft, sweet words
that are only spoken by true lovers,
throughout the ages, in all tongues,
our spirits have reappeared
--we have lived on and on!

We are the love odes of old
And the ballads that chronicle
the joys and the pain of love,
of separation and union of lovers.
--We are every love that's ever been!

If I stare at you long enough
I know your ancient images will emerge;
I will see you clad in gown and flowers
With the light of time shining from your hair.
--You are the image of what is remembered forever!

Two Sunsets

I sent to you two Sunsets,
Many days ago,
You were to view them one day,
When your spirits were feeling low.

But now my need is great,
I can use them both right now;
Please let me view the colors,
Of clouds Astral-endowed.

This Note

I placed this note
Inside a bottle and threw it
way out to sea:
"I am here, waiting,
Please come to me."

Are you the one,
that I was thinking of
way back then?
If you were, tell me,
"Yes, I am thee."

The Woman I Love

The woman I love was born to me
seven months ago.

She is in every room of my house
and I can see her,
and smell her, and feel her
in there every day.

It is like she fills every space
of my life everywhere I look.

I saw her once, backlit by the sun,
standing naked, at a window,
looking out at the rising sun.

That vision has stayed with me
like a favorite photograph.

It will be, like an image frozen
on a screen, remain forever in me.

I remember a gift she gave me
once with violet Irises on it
and violet ribbons. I took the irises
and ribbons off the box
and placed them in her hair.
I see her that way still,

in bloom, in violet.

She is always in motion.
In some rooms I see a blur,
Because she moves so quickly,
but I can see her smile.
I can always see her smile.
But, can I stop her from
Moving on in her life,
out of my life, and on to another?

Your Presence

Your presence follows me,
Through the day everywhere.
No mere apparition,
You are the spirit,
And the soul that I share.

Though you dwell everyday,
In your own body too,
I feel you in me,
Reciting to my heart,
All day long, "I love you."

This Day

This day will never come again,
And we have only so many days,
Like this my friend.

Will we use it to talk and laugh,
To sing and dance at every chance?
Or to make love?

Will we linger a little longer in bed,
Or rise to despise the day instead,
Your wish my dear?

Or will we be reckless in the open air,
Seen by anyone, savoring the fun,
On this day my friend.

Together

Together we're one,
the sum of two,
though we have traveled
in tandem solitude,
like dancers, moving to rhythm,
right on cue.

Waiting

Waiting?

Yes, for many years now.

Hopeful?

Yes, all that my tears allow.

Perfect?

No, the glory is missing here.

Defect?

No, it's the years that interfere.

The Look

The look you give to me at times,
Seems to say so many things,
About the love you feel for me,
And how much happiness it brings.

The look is different at different times,
But what doesn't ever change,
Is how it conveys so much love,
Lead-heavy and lavish in its range.

That look may pass between us,
Whether alone or in a crowded room;
It doesn't matter where we are,
I know the look and know it is for whom!

It Is Night

It is night. I lay beside the woman
that I never thought I would ever meet.
But, somehow at long last I have found her!

My thoughts drift to the world outside.
I hear cars along the road speeding
on their way toward their own lives.
Do they know how happy I am?
I want them to know.
I want the whole world to know.
I want to stop the people in the cars
and tell them: I have found her!

Yes, I have found the woman
who is beautiful to me.
She is as beautiful as Helen of Troy,
as Juliet, as every beauty who's ever lived.
And she is here beside me.
I am blissful and contented.
I can go to sleep and know
that I cannot dream of a more
beautiful woman than she is.
Beauty and love have been granted me.

The fullest measure of each.

I am blessed.

It is night, it is right!

Does The Heart

Does the heart grow old?
You might say, "Yes, as a muscle must."
I mean *the heart* as the spirit's central part.
You reply, "Yes, it grows weary with distrust."

Does the heart grow strong with the exercise of love?
You would say, "You're wrong, that's just abject lust."

I point out many have proved my point.
You reply, "Yes, but many more have gone bust"

Let me change your mind by example over time.
"Yes, but it will take a long time to readjust."

But I say, that is all we have to alter us.
You reply, "Then I'm sorry for all my distrust."

I Did Not

I did not ever doubt,
that one glorious, glamorous night,
I would finally meet you, again.
I would often see you there,
where I first saw you dear,
rising, like a flower in bloom.

We would meet, as we have met,
over and over again, in my dreams,
and in my heart, over and over, again.

That Day

That day was friendly
as you and I smiled
on a picture-postcard kind of day.
Will you be kind and friendly
and just as clearly caring
as on that sunny Summer day?
I could not imagine you
any other way.

It Recently Dawned On Me

It recently dawned on me, dramatically, how thoroughly you are attached to my universe, while standing in a check-out line at the grocery store and looking at the things I had in my cart: toiletries and food, books and clothes, gifts and miscellaneous things --how each item selected was selected with you in mind; either because I thought you would like it or because I wanted to please you-- and how I had considered each item now with you in mind, bought somehow a part of you.

Touch

Do I touch you
when I touch you?

Do you feel
when you feel me?

Do I sense all
that can sense me?

Do you tell me when
when I am there?

It Is Time

It is time for us to do it right,
to take long walks with the one
we love in the night.
Then take their hand
and promise them
love forevermore,
--and then give more,
In every way, every day,
and let our love pour,
on to each other,
and not let there be another;
And to try harder than we ever did before.

We can pretend we were rehearsing then,
with all those others,
and all those times before;
but now everything's in sight for us to finally,
and precisely, do it right,
now and forevermore.

We Sleep Together

We sleep together well,
you and I.

we can safely relax in sleep,
and breathe our restful breaths in deep,
curled into each other's bodies.

When can I feel content again?
I feel it each night I sleep with you.

I Once Loved

I once loved to read books past my bedtime,
under the covers, using a small penlight.

Maybe that's why I always think of you in bed,
just like a book and enjoy you every night.

I open you to a good place, enjoy each page,
and I love how the book turns out.

What

What we've shared will be
forever with me
evermore.

It Is In The Morning

It is in the morning
That I feel most alive,
Especially after a night
Spent loving you.
I can start the day aware
Of how much love we have to share,
And how much more I want to live,
All because of only you.

I Want to Show

I want to show my love
In every way I can.

Buy you presents every week?
Of course I can.

And remember to call?
I'll be punctual and sweet.

Change your oil? Check your tires?
Agree, yessiree, and done!

Just remember to wear lace,
and show me a happy face
even when you've heard that story
a million times before.
That's how you'll score.

About The Author

Ian Lewis

He is an award-winning author of short stories and flash fiction. His fiction has been published online and in print by Amazon.com. He has authored books of poetry, collections of short stories, and a novel, Inpersonal. He also co-wrote and edited women's stories of love and life with Iris Mede.